Best Wishes,
Brandy Alexander

Think of me when
you read these
loving words —
Jerry
2-14-94

1

HEARTSTRINGS

HEARTSTRINGS

by
BRANDY ALEXANDER

Published
by
Sealed With A Kiss
Illinois-1992

Library of Congress Cataloging in Publication Data

Alexander, Brandy.
  Heartstrings
    p.   cm.
  1. Love poetry, American.   1. Title

PS3551.L3485H4   811'.54—dc20
ISBN: 0-9624227-1-1
Library of Congress Catalog Card Number 91-62159

PRINTED IN THE
UNITED STATES OF AMERICA

THANK YOU

B.A.
S.P.
Patricia Woods
for graciously offering the photographs
that appear on these pages

M.V.
for meeting all my lithographic needs
with a smile

Marijo Hobbs
for insight and imagination

Ed Liedy
for a wealth of knowledge and information

Photri-Photo Research International
for the cover photo

Special thanks to my sister Belinda who will always be my hero and the wind beneath my wings. And who's life is the testament and inspiration for the title of this book.

*Dedicated to those couples who know
that eternity's clock has no hands,
and the heart's eternal hourglass
never runs out of sand.*

A NOTE FROM THE AUTHOR

Sooner or later
we all believe in love,
not as a whim
but out of human necessity.

Sooner or later
the soul
believes in the unbelievable.
It is not wise
to be so self-assured
that no form of human kindness
can reach us.

Sooner or later
we all believe in love.

Contents

HEARTSTRINGS

PRIVATE CORRIDORS

There is a side
Within you
Where I alone have been.
At the outer reaches of your heart...somewhere
Beautiful smiles
And secrets you've cherished
Since you were eager
And twenty
And believing in love at first sight.

Words can't always say enough,
And some feelings are just too profound
Or revealing
To be expressed,
Maybe only
When we're alone.

There is a side
Within you
Where I alone have been
Where you have never taken another,
Or ever will.

ECSTASY

Give me the kind of love I can feel
Make a joyful noise unto my senses
Raise the roof
Tear the house down
Bring forth the thunder and lightning
I want to hear firecrackers and sirens
Let my heart swing from the chandelier
And shout like in church on Sunday morning.

THE DIARY

Many call love a color
That paints the very soul.
Many call love an ember
That burns then turns cold.
Many call love a gamble
Just an unlucky roll
I call love a story
And you its' only scroll.

It's the eyes afraid of looking
That never learn to see.
It's the wish afraid of being granted
That never comes to be.
It's the one who holds too close
That never learns to let go,
And the mind afraid of thinking
That never learns to know.

When the day has been too weary
And seems to never end,
And you feel that love is only
Someone elses friend;
Never forget in the solitude
Deep beneath the pain and debris
Lies the scroll that with the writer's pen
In the end becomes the diary.

EXTRA SENSUOUS PERCEPTION

There is a very special part of me
that I only let you touch
on those rare occasions
when God is smiling in heaven
and all is right with the world.

...It is the same special part
that you touch that touches you
even when you're not here.

LOCHINVAR

I know he doesn't know me...
After all we never even met
But out there is a man
Whose memory I've kept in a diary...
Not the kind I'd keep in a dresser drawer
...Or up in the attic
But tightly in my soul
Where I keep all the love letters I meant to write
...But somehow never did.

And yet...I want to know him
But I know I never will...
So content I'll be
...On rainy days
Whenever I'm home alone
To secretly read those pages deep within.

COMPANIONSHIP

In appreciation of all who have fancied me in their
   souls,
With gratitude and love. Deep
      gratitude to all
Who strolled the beaches with me
To hear the waves upon the ocean
Then each would exit, each one down his
   own separate street
Or to other arms, a deeper love.
But he, who, in my wildest dream
Made me a believer of love in spite of myself,
Dared to whisper what I always knew
   in my heart of hearts.
The outer reaches of my soul say thanks!
When old I sit before the fireplace many years from now,
      I will know
Everything is nothing if you have no one.

SONIC BOOM

Lips wet with fire
Kisses that could melt snow
Bodies as steamy as dry ice
Love that could shatter granite
You and I were on a collision course
Somewhere in the heat of it all
Our hearts collided and became one

NIGHT MUSIC

The feel of you against my heart
It's warm where you're touching me
You reach that secret place...
We enter the eye of the hurricane
Every breath we take takes us over the edge,
As our hearts sing in acappella
An old familiar tune.

THE GUY IN THE BROOKS BROTHERS SHIRT

Old lovers carved their initials on my heart...
Every memory of each
Is slightly out of focus
From the one before
Like dust that has settled
On a camera lens.
Each photo hazy...

And yet...each was gallant
Each won my heart
In his own special way...
I remember them all now with watercolors
But I remember you most of all.

INNER SEDUCTION

Who are you
that I've come to slumber with
like this...you
who enter my bed
with restless passion?

You say you've touched me
in that secret place?...That
in searching for ecstasy
I formed a bond
and loved time after time
those whom I never loved
before?

What utter madness it is
that you should give me permission
into your heart...When
the heart of the lovers
for whom these pages were written
have locked the door and
thrown away the key forever.

And who am I
to fight fate?

ILLUSIONS

We spend years building walls
that we think no one can penetrate
    until love finally arrives.
All our man-made dragons
  then vanish in a puff of smoke.

FOR PASSION'S SAKE

If you must desire me, let it be for nothing
Except for passion's sake only. Don't say
You love me for my sense of humor, my beauty,
  my way
Of whispering softly in the night
For these things in themselves, darling,
  may
Be altered, or I may alter them in time for you,
  and
Passion will be no more. Neither want me
  for
Your own ego to place me as a trophy
Upon the mantle,
For I might turn and go and lose your love
  suddenly;
But let your passions melt my heart
Like April snow, that even then
You might see eternity in my eyes.

WARM TO THE TOUCH

I feel your warmth
around me
like hot tea on a winter night;
soothing,
steamy,
putting me in the mood.

You are the only pullover
my heart will ever need
to keep me
safe and secure
from life's shivering winds

SPONTANEITY

In the soft darkness
I memorize the room:
A heart-shaped bed
Night table with photo
Clothes in disarray.

In the wee small hours of morning
We are two hearts on the brink of passion
I feel your velvet warmth
Our love will keep for a long time.

INTIMATE MOMENTS

Two lovers running to escape from all the
Cares of the day,
We always end up coming back
To our peaceful hideaway...

To kick our shoes off and unwind,
And wrap up in each other like
Ribbons wrapped around presents
At Christmas time.

NO ULTERIOR MOTIVES

No strings attached
is just another way of
letting go

As long as I give you
your freedom
...I let
go

Be the you that you want to be
...My independence is independent
upon yours
and

If we choose to be together
...We have joint custody
of this love

MAKING IT THE OLD FASHIONED WAY

...It is not by some toss of a coin
that we get closer to each other
as we grow older...Especially
when we were afraid
we wouldn't

They said we wouldn't last
    Yet...
We are more fact than fiction...
Angels do smile down from heaven
from time to time...
But most of all
Hard work pays off

LONELINESS

For as long as you've been gone
I've been dreaming
of your homecoming

Every day I listen
for the turn of your key...I wonder
who the terminally ill in hospitals
wait for

You might not have stayed
away so long
if you had known...
(But missing someone
like crazy is not
suppose to be chic)
Each dance with the
piper must be paid for
(Wanting to or not)...Loneliness
isn't perfect
It is still the heart's
way of bouncing a check

GOING THE DISTANCE

It takes a kiss when alone on an elevator together
Holding hands under the table when out to dinner
The warm touch of arms holding tight
Eyes meeting in a special way from across a crowded room
It takes real guts to make love work
Many have left/Few have stayed

CONVICTIONS

With your love,
You have sanded my heart smooth.
Yours is a love that's sure and safe;
A secure fortress away from all of life's storms.
You are moments of deep joy,
And quiet laughter.
You have lost yourself in me,
And me in you.
There is nothing that our love cannot change.

HOLDING OUT

Sometimes the Gods smile
And you awake with someone
that you want to
wake up with for
the rest of your life.

It is right as rain
The perfect signal for our
moving forward...I open my heart
and touch him with
my love...He responds back
to me...And changes the future
forever.

It is a miracle
(one that would make front page news)
There is some kind of poetic
justice in falling in love
for the last time the
first time you fall.

Always thought it would be this way...But
there was once a moment
when I almost traded the diamonds
in for cut glass
...Luckily, I
didn't

MAGIC OF THE NIGHT

A silent time of two hearts beating
The explosion of breaths taken/
We are the music in the dark
The unspoken words/
Arms reaching out in silent rapture
Suspending us between time and space.

A FAMILIAR PRESENCE

The nearness between us
is consummate and
free...We are
brought together by
a conviction...Still

You knew I would never leave
(I'm glad you asked me
to stay)

It must be reassuring
(when you think about it)
to know we have
each other...Than if
we had someone else...After all

We know where all the
skeletons are hid in
each others' closet

INTERRUPTED HEART BEATS

It's a feeling
Somewhere between the throat and chest
When you hear yourself silently saying:
'Be still my heart'

It's there when you least expect,
Like roller coaster rides
Can bring it about
When you're falling through space

And scary movies
Can do it
When you know any moment
The monster will appear

And yes, even you
Like a surprise birthday party
Can still make my heart beat
One moment and
Stand still the next

UNREQUITED LOVE

I love you in a time where there are no
alarm clocks
watches
schedules
dates
red circles around days on calendars

I love you in a place where there are no
walls
bars
chains
burglar alarms
locks on doors

A REALIZATION

Yours are the
lips I've come to kiss
like this...Yours
are the love notes
written on my
heart

You are the one I
watch the sun rise with...That
in giving of myself
I mold a love that
will always be for the taking.

It is a lucky twist of fate
That you should give me entrance
into the private corridors of your
mind...When the other lovers
(of whom I think of now)
never granted me such a
luxury.

DEPENDABILITY

You are a calm in a world gone mad
You shelter me from life's storms
You illuminate my universe
With the sunshine of your love,
Teaching my heart to sing
Even in the darkness.

LOVERS REMAIN

Lovers remain
...There isn't any
big mystery to this
...It is just that way
But you must be brave
to say that
you always
want them
to

...Rarely lovers
leave...But
that never
means they
really wanted
to go

There are a few lovers
who always find
their way back home
They never lost
their key...Because

Lovers really never say
good-bye

OLD FAMILIAR FEELINGS

I look deep past your gaze and
See the reflection of my own unbridled passions
Your kiss has lit a fire in my heart
As silver fingers of moonlight caress the night,
Your bedroom eyes undress me.
We'll make our own forever
As you love me again for the first time.

HOMECOMING

Love is asleep now in a great somewhere,
Where we haven't been in a long time.
All our midnight whispers have gone to a silent place.
It has been such a long time since we tried
To squeeze the last ounce of passion out of one another.

...I can hardly wait
to be your lover once again.

THE GOOD WIFE

Another trip out of town
...I'll stay back
See that the home fires
are kept burning

Hurry back
I'll keep your side
of the bed warm...Never
can get use to these
good-byes

I'll be all right
...I've often wondered what it's like
being married to the man who's
job keeps him away from home

Bring me back a souvenir
...I'll say a silent prayer
in the darkness tonight
I'll even save you the last
slice of apple pie

For now...I'll stay back
See that the home fires
are kept burning

THOSE WHO LOVE THE MOST

Those who love the most
From early on/to the grave
Their wills are made of cast iron
Their hearts are always giving intensive care
They wrote the book on strength

These are the volunteers who work in soup kitchens/
These are the little old ladies who always leave
Bread crumbs in the backyard for robins/
No one goes left unfed

These are the children that kneel at bedtime to pray/
These are the widows who go to church to light candles/
They know God always listens

As time is measured/love goes on forever
It is an old cliche that pen and paper
Would never do justice to/
Except you always know it is so.
There is a tomorrow in every today.
There is celebration in us all/
This is how we come to separate lovers
From mere one-night-stands

There are people who will love you even if you
Meet them ten years from today/
There will always be a place in their heart for you,
They can breathe vitality into your soul.
Those who love the most
As time is measured/you are one of them

BEGINNINGS

I did live my whole long life
   to get to this moment
      in time
to be told by your devilish smile
   that I am loved more than
      I ever thought I would be

I came hoping to find
   a way to spend the summer
yet it became more special than any summer before
   Now to leave the 'us' we have become
      would be a tragic contradiction
      Hello is always
   sweeter than good-bye

OPTIMISM

There is always the lover in us
That wants one to one and
One on one
In each others' arms
There is safety here
For to believe in love
Makes lovers of us all

A DOZEN ROSES

A dozen roses arrived today
Unexpected...along with a card

I ran my fingers across
The letters on the envelope
That spelled out my name
And smelled
The scent of your after-shave

Ah...Such a sweet surprise as this
welcomed...
putting me in the mood...

And yet after last night's fight...
Your way of saying sorry...
You always did know my weak spot

FOREVER

A look from across a crowded room,
Can still make my heart skip a beat.
An inside joke that only we know the punch line to,
Still brings a quiet smile.
As rivers keep on flowing,
As clouds still float on high,
Some things are deeper than time.

THE REQUEST

This poem is a
request

We are
parents now...And
yet we were lovers
first...So

this poem was written
with the hope
that our marriage
might lift us out
of our parenthood
one day

This is not to
understand how come
we love each other
But only
....How much

This poem is a
request

HOW LONG WILL LOVE LAST?

Love is a memory.
  A memory is two lives touching
    in a special way;
The deeper the touch,
  the longer the memory;
The longer the memory,
  the greater the love;
I am in constant battle with Time
  for this memory;
I will fight as long
  as I treasure this memory;

I will love as long as the darkroom within
    my brain continues to develop this memory;
If during the course of my life,
    I stop loving you,
    conclude that Time was a better opponent than I;
But if during my last hour with life,
    I am still loving you,
    only conclude that I wanted the memory
    much more than Time.

A CONSUMING PASSION

I have come as close
as body and heart can bring me
to you.
I have journeyed, loved
dreamed a hundred times in sleep
seeing your face in my mind's eye.

We have learned to make each other laugh.
I sometimes think
we haven't been together long enough
to enjoy such a luxury,
still the nearness that creates the magic
is so real
that we seem destined to be.

LOVE LET US BE KIND

Love let us be kind...
Let us give unto each other
The sympathy we offer strangers.
Let us have the insight to see
The differences in each of us and
In so seeing these differences
Pull closer together
Not farther apart.
Surely, we want each other
(for there is fire in our blood!)
But certainly we do not need each other,
This is the beginning of wisdom.

SPEND THE NIGHT

If you spend the night
I know you will not
Want to leave come morning
So please...
Stay

And yes
You can sleep on the side
By the window...
I'll let the moonlight in
I'll serve you breakfast in bed

If you stay...
Admit it
Your heart unpacked hours ago

So please...
Just spend the night
And see that much can be said in the silence
After all...
You can be the lullaby
That rocks my heart to sleep tonight

LONGEVITY

One of the things
I found
When you fell in love
With me,
Was the courage
Of your convictions
To stay

BLANK VERSE

It started the day we met.
I didn't know just how much
I was going to love you,
Until the first time we made love.

I try sometimes to say just
How I feel,
But the words get caught in my throat.
Maybe I'll come across
Some great line of poetry one day
To express it all
Till then
I guess these will have to do.

IN A PAST LIFE

I knew you
even before we met
We were friends
turned lovers

At our first meeting
I was one up
on you
I had read the
last chapter
even before you read
the first...Yet

I had to play
hard-to-get...Since

Before we had met
I knew you even then

FLAMES OF PASSIONS

The neatly made bed our love making unmade...
Our love is here
In every pillow crease,
In every wrinkle of the sheet

Love light gleams in our eyes...
Our hearts beat as one
Every time our lips meet,
Every time we melt into each other's embrace
Every time
Every time
Every time

WHEN LOVE TAKES OVER

The first time you loved me, you but only loved
The mind of me wherewith I think;
And ever since, my thoughts grew more clear and
I begin to realize that time spent
With you is not lost. The second time
You loved me, you but only loved
The heart of me wherewith I feel;
And ever since, my feelings grew more intense
As your love made over what needed
Making over. The third time
You loved me, you loved
The soul of me wherewith
I am linked to eternity;
And ever since, you've become someone to come
Home to again and again,
As we are never apart for so long that
There is no getting back.

HOMEWARD BOUND

I'm one step from your arms
I'm two steps from your kiss
I've come too far
Take me in unto your heart and
Throw away the key forevermore

IN LOVE'S EMBRACE

Beads of sweat line our faces
Flames of passion burn in our eyes
Our hearts beat at a whirlwind pace
As our bodies dance through the night sky

CHOICES

Some people stay together
for the time of their lives (today)

Some people stay together
for a time in their life (tomorrow)

Some people stay together
for a lifetime (forever)

LOVE'S CHALLENGE

Why not demand it all?
Life is too short
to settle for less.
The trick is to leave
space in our plans
so that the magic
can happen...Still

We have no magic potions
that will give us perfection.
Sure love may have brought
us together
but we will have to do
the staying.

THE JOURNEY

Let's go sit under the stars
you and I, arms around each other, on the lake
...at daybreak, above our laughter, hear the birds.
Let's look at the sun,
rejoicing, warming our faces;

Let's walk together toward the park
Where the trees stretch on forever
In a summer beyond the seasons
I want to take you with me to eternity.

STILL LIFE

We are apart for now,
Not because we want to be
But because we have to...
And sure, we're both homesick,
But not for the ocean-view condo,
Only for love's quiet celebration.

The heart has a memory
Just like the mind

WHO SAID LOVE IS BLIND?

Words are not necessary when love is present
There is this silent communication between us.
We have a love that touches so deep
That even in total darkness we find each other.
We have become a kind of
Blind man's bluff played among lovers,
Reading in braille the secret code
Written upon each others' heart.

YOUR LOVE IS...

Your love is...
Cozy as an easy chair at the end of the day
Rich as the pot of gold at the end of the rainbow
And ever close, just a heart beat away.

Your love is...
Silent as new falling snow
Radiant as the sun's pure passion
And impulsive as the moon's unfailing glow.

FOR KEEPS

We have said much
We have loved often
Our love has put down roots.
Nourished on our convictions,
All that stays is also all that remains;
And our joy will not be worn away by time

I.D.

Do tell me the name written on your heart
Who walks down the canyons of your mind
What you like to do on Valentine's Day...
Your favorite Chablis...
Your soul's combination...

You are more than just a number
In a little black book,
You are one of love's vital statistics.

BLIND FAITH

I can tell from the look that's in your eyes,
You've never been out this far before.
You've been saving your heart for a rainy day,
But somehow you always managed to get rained upon.
Step out and walk across the tightrope of love.
I'll be your net.
I'll hold your hand.
I won't let you fall.

LOVE

Each love is proclaimed a star in the
  heavens;
Yet what heart cares, beats a
  little faster.
But all the lovers around
In all the parked cars with bated
  breath
For their plight, down to the last
  star,
Illuminates brightly in the moonlight;
Love echoes love across the
  universe,
By common threads of magic.
I think this unexplained passion which stirs
A lover's heart, I think this
Eternal cry, when first
  begun
Let us all realize that holding back
Love is the only pain that can
Make the heart ache.

LOVE'S RIDDLE

Untasted honey is the sweetest kind
Always was
Always will be
Take the beat but not my heart
Somethings are better not had than had...

And even as the moon suspended
In the sky looks alone,
It still is attached to the heavens.
If, my darling, you can remember this
The stars will write our name.

COMMITMENT

We have the kind of love
Every woman dreams of
And every man dreams about

...full of promises
and possibilities

No room for doubt
This is our moment...

Together
We are more
than what we were
singular

DIRECTIONS

So, in the end,
It is this that must be said:
Do not mistake what our love is/
It is our relationship and
In that relationship all that truly counts
Is what we may become/
Become not only to each other but
To ourselves as well,
For from this all else proceeds.